BLOOMFIELD TOWNSHIP PUBLIC LIBRARY
3 1160 00352 4332

W9-CNA-329

# Dogs Everywhere

by Cor Hazelaar

Alfred A. Knopf New York

For Nina and Larry, who are always so helpful

THIS IS A BORZOI BOOK PUBLISHED BY ALFRED A. KNOPF, INC.


Published in the United States of America by Alfred A. Knopf, Inc., New York, and simultaneously
in Canada by Random House of Canada Limited, Toronto. Distributed by Random House, Inc., New York.

Library of Congress Cataloging-in-Publication Data
Hazelaar, Cor.
Dogs everywhere / by Cor Hazelaar. p. cm.
Summary: Describes dogs being walked in the park.
ISBN 0-679-85439-8 (trade) ISBN 0-679-95439-2 (lib. bdg.)
[1. Dog walking—Fiction. 2. Dogs—Fiction.] I. Title.
PZ7.H3149674Do 1995 [E]—dc20 93-32597

Manufactured in Singapore 10 9 8 7 6 5 4 3 2 1

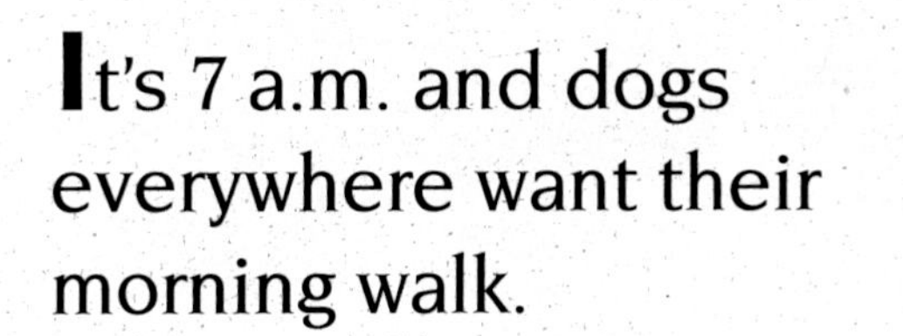

It's 7 a.m. and dogs everywhere want their morning walk.

They wait at the door.
It's time to go out!

They smell the trees and grass as they race to the park.

There is so much to see
and hear and do!

Some dogs, if they are very well behaved, are allowed off their leashes.

They meet their
friends,
exchange scents
and secrets,
and plot and plan.

They dig! And splash! And run!

They imagine they are wild like their ancestors,

chasing caribou across the tundra.

Until their hunt is cut short by the calls
and whistles of their masters.

It's time to go in.

Back at home, they eat and sleep and wait…

…until evening brings their masters' return…

…and walk time! At last!

Back in the park, they celebrate.

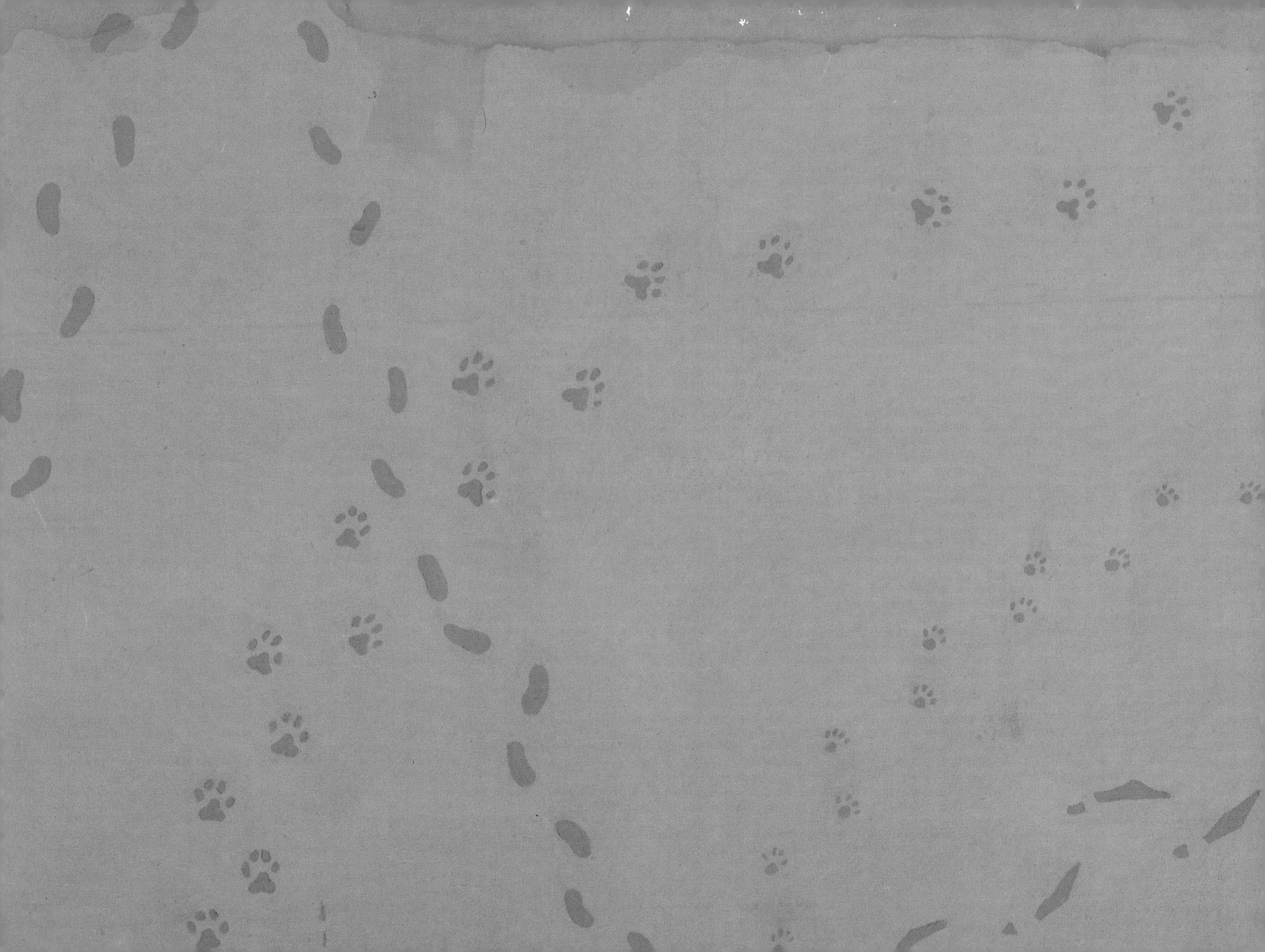